Beneath the Waves

Two Ghost Stories

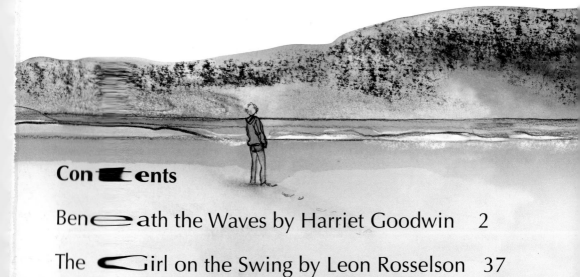

Contents

Illustrated by Helen Van Vliet and Jimothy Oliver

Beneath the Waves

by Harriet Goodwin

Chapter 1

Joe shut the door to the little room and threw his bag down
on the bed.

Of all the places they could have come on holiday,
Dad had to go and choose this one. It was totally rubbish.
There was no amusement arcade. No pier. No shops.
Apart from the hotel they were staying in, there were only
a few houses and an ancient-looking church. Oh, and
some wreck of an old monastery, all stern grey stone and
crumbling arches.

It had to be about the most boring holiday destination in the world.

As far as he could tell, the only reason they were here at all was that they'd holidayed in the same village when he was a little boy. Stayed in the same hotel, even. It was just as he remembered it, Dad said. Hadn't changed a bit.

Joe sank down on to the bed and sighed.

So the *place* hadn't changed, maybe. But just about everything else had. Since Mum had died his entire life had changed, and to him nothing would ever be the same again.

He glanced out of the window at the windswept beach. Mum had loved it here, apparently. She'd always planned to come back some day, but of course she never had. Because of her illness, she'd never got the chance. And now he was here instead, stuck for a whole week in the middle of nowhere with only Dad for company.

Joe swallowed back the tightness in his throat.

If only Dad would stop talking about her the whole time, it wouldn't be so bad. It had been a complete nightmare on the way down in the car. He'd gone on and on about all the things Mum had liked about the place: her favourite walks around the village, her favourite food in the hotel, even her favourite flavour of ice cream.

Didn't Dad realise how it stirred everything up for him? Joe just didn't want to know. It was easier to push anything to do with Mum right to the back of his mind. Somehow it hurt less that way.

Joe stood up from the bed and frowned at his reflection in the mirror.

Dad had said he wanted to walk down to the beach before dinner. Taste the sea air and blow away a few cobwebs after the long journey down.

Well, he didn't want to taste the sea air or blow away the stupid cobwebs. All he wanted was to go back home to London and spend the summer hanging out with his mates. Surely that wasn't too much to ask?

Chapter 2

Whatever Dad was playing at, it certainly made him look pretty silly.

He'd acted normally enough when they were walking down the path to the beach, but then when they'd reached the beginning of the shingle he'd started to pace towards the sea in slow, deliberate strides, muttering to himself as he went.

Joe looked on, bemused. At least there was no one watching. It was getting on for seven o'clock and the beach was completely deserted. All the holiday-makers must have packed up and headed home ages ago. In any case, the sky was clouding over and there was a definite chill in the air.

"What are you doing, Dad?" he called, running down the beach after him. "Have you gone completely mad?"

His dad didn't answer. He continued to stride down the beach in a dead straight line, holding up his hand as if he didn't want to be interrupted.

At last he stopped. "Twenty!" he exclaimed triumphantly. "I'm sure that's right. I'm sure that's what she used to do."

He looked round as Joe drew to a halt beside him. "It was part of a game your mum played with you when we came here before," he explained. "I don't expect you remember."

Joe glanced away.

"She had this special patch of beach, you see," his dad went on. "She used to take your hand at the end of the path and count out the steps – 20 of her big strides to 40 of your little ones." He smiled to himself. "Then she'd spread out the towels and plaster you in suncream, and when she'd done that she'd tell you to turn away and close your eyes while she buried things in the shingle."

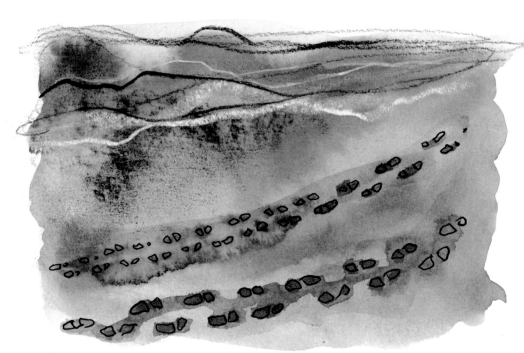

"*Buried* things?" echoed Joe in spite of himself. "What for?"

"For you to find, of course," replied his dad. "It was a great game. You used to screech out loud every time you found something in amongst the pebbles."

There was a short silence.

"What kind of things did she hide?" asked Joe at last.

"Oh, all sorts," replied his dad. "Keys. Coins. Anything she could find in her handbag, really." He laughed. "I remember one time she buried a pair of earrings. A couple of tiny golden moons. You found one of them almost at once, but none of us could find the other, no matter how hard we searched. Not that your mum minded. She said it would most likely be washed out to sea one day and the mermaids would have it. You know what she was like. Never let anything upset her. Always looked on the bright side."

Joe swallowed. He began to walk towards the sea.

"Where d'you think you're off to?" his dad called after him. "You can't go swimming in this, you know. It's way too choppy." He pointed to where a series of ominous-looking clouds was fast gathering on the horizon. "There's a storm coming in. Just look at the colour of that sky."

Joe rolled his eyes. "I'm not going *in*, Dad," he called back over his shoulder. "I just want to chuck a few stones in the water, that's all. There's no one else around."

"Well, can't we do it together? We could have a bit of a contest, if you like. See which of us can throw the furthest."

Joe shook his head. "I'd rather be on my own, thanks. If it's all the same with you."

"Suit yourself," replied his dad, shrugging. "I'll sit down and wait for you here. Don't be long though. The hotel starts serving fish and chips at seven."

Joe walked on towards the shore.

Right now, he didn't feel in the least bit hungry.
All that talk about Mum had ruined his appetite. And he
didn't feel much like standing around on a freezing cold
beach chucking stones into the sea either. Already the wind
was getting up and goose bumps were appearing on
his arms. But he'd had to find a way of getting away from
Dad, if only for a few minutes. If he had to listen to any more
of Dad's memories, he reckoned he'd probably scream.

He glanced over his shoulder to where his dad was now
sitting on the special patch of beach – his *mum's* special
patch of beach. It was such a weird thought, knowing she'd
once sat there, playing some childish game in the shingle.

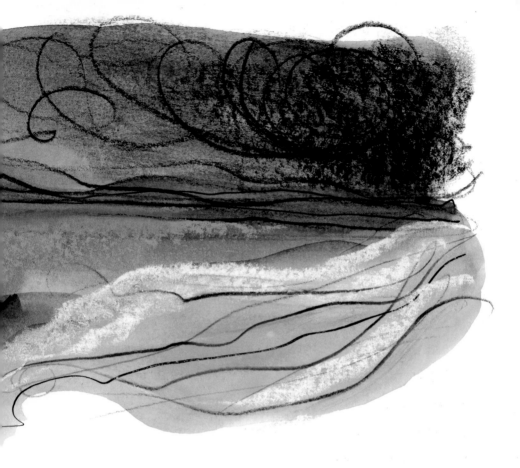

How he wished she was here, messing about on
the beach with him. Even with the weather closing in on
them like this, she'd have found a way to make it fun.
What Dad had said was true; Mum *had* always looked on
the bright side of everything. And he tried to do the same.
It was just so hard when a dark cloud seemed to hang over
him wherever he went, just like the ones he could see now,
looming over the great grey sea.

Joe picked up a smooth, flat pebble and threw it into the water. Not much chance of any decent skimming this evening. Not with the sea as rough as this. There was a storm on the way all right. And a pretty bad one at that.

He frowned. In amongst the whistling of the wind and the crashing of the waves, he could hear something strange – something that sounded a bit like music or bells. He stepped back, dodging a wave that was rushing towards him, then tilted his head to one side in an effort to catch the noise again – but it had gone.

Joe sighed. He must be imagining things. It was probably just the sound of the waves churning up the shingle.

He glanced at his watch. Seven o'clock already. It was time he got back to Dad.

He cast another pebble into the sea and watched as it arched over the heaving waves and disappeared beneath the surface – and then he turned and began to make his way up the beach.

15

Chapter 3

That night, the storm tore in from the sea.

Joe tossed and turned in bed, listening as the wind screamed over the rooftops and horizontal sheets of rain rattled against the window panes. Through the gap in the curtains, electric-white flashes of lightning illuminated the sea as it surged under a blanket of thick black cloud.

By morning the worst was over, but a thin rain still fell, cloaking the village in grey.

Joe pulled up the hood of his anorak and followed his dad out of the hotel entrance.

It didn't look like today was going to be much fun. Dad's idea of indoor holiday entertainment seemed to amount to nothing more than a trip to the local museum.

He scuffed his trainers against the pavement.

Until now he hadn't even noticed the museum. It was just a few doors down from the hotel, but so tiny you'd only have to blink to miss it.

"Of course we'd always meant to pay it a visit when we came here before," his dad was saying. "Your mum read somewhere that the village was absolutely steeped in history."

Joe groaned to himself. History? *History?* How boring could you get? Their first full day down here and he was going to be dragged around a museum. It was worse than being at school. At least there he had his mates to talk to. All he had here was Dad.

"But in the end," his dad went on, "we reckoned you were a bit young to take any of it in. Besides, we had fabulous weather that week. I don't think there was a cloud in the sky the whole holiday. There was no need to spend any time indoors." He unlatched a small black gate and led the way into the museum.

They paid their entrance fee and wandered into the first of the exhibition rooms, its stuffy darkness already crowded with a gaggle of tourists studying a large white information board.

Joe's eyes flitted over the text.

Incredible as it might sound, this village was once a great city, covering over a square kilometre of land. In medieval times it was a vibrant port, full of houses and churches and hospitals, as well as many magnificent buildings, including a royal palace.

"Your mum would have loved this," his dad whispered. "She was always so interested in the past. She – "

"Dad!" exclaimed Joe. "Will you *stop* going on about Mum all the time? It's totally doing my head in." His dad gaped at him. "I don't want to know what she was interested in, OK? I don't want to know anything except why you had to bring me here on holiday in the first place."

There was a very long silence.

The tourists had stopped studying the information board and were staring at them, their mouths hanging open. Then they all began to talk at once and hurried out into the next room, leaving Joe and his dad by themselves.

Joe looked down at the floor, fighting back the tears that threatened to spill from his eyes. "I'm sorry," he muttered. "I – I didn't mean it to come out like that." He bit his lip. "It's just that you're always talking about her and sometimes – "

"Please," interrupted his dad, "don't apologise." He reached out and touched Joe lightly on the arm. "It's me who should be saying sorry." He ran his fingers through his hair. "I'll tell you what," he said, "let's get round this museum double-quick and then drive into town. We could go and watch that film you've been wanting to see. How does that sound?"

Joe shrugged and nodded.

"Good," said his dad, "that's settled then." He started to move away. "Now – you try and enjoy the museum. I won't get in your way, I promise. I'll go on ahead and meet you outside when you're ready."

Joe waited until his dad had disappeared, then let out a long sigh.

He glanced around the little room, taking it in for the first time. The walls were covered with more information boards, just like the one he'd already read, but at the far end there was something that looked a bit more promising: a small cinema screen with a couple of chairs in front of it. Going over, he pressed the button beneath the screen and sat down. Almost at once a black and white sketch of the town appeared and a soundtrack crackled into life.

"Imagine how this place must have been in its heyday, humming with the sounds of a thriving city. Imagine the hustle and bustle of the streets, the cries of the market-traders, the boats sailing in and out of the harbour."

The picture gave way to another drawing, this time of a stormy sea, not unlike the scene he'd glimpsed from the window the previous night.

"But everything was about to change. In the 13th century a series of terrible storms devastated the town. Many buildings, including the palace and all but one of its churches, were swept into the sea. Gradually the river silted up and the town became the tiny village that exists today."

Again the picture changed, and Joe found himself staring at a modern-day clip of divers wading out to sea and helicopters circling overhead.

"The murky depths have been trawled on a number of occasions, in the hope of recovering some token of the lost city, but nothing has ever been found. It seems that the sea took everything into its thieving grasp."

The voice droned on, but Joe had stopped listening.

He slumped down in his chair. He should never have snapped at Dad like that, especially not in front of all those tourists. It was totally out of order. But he hadn't been able to help himself. It was as if his feelings had just exploded out of him, like a cork popping from a bottle.

He stood up. He'd had enough of this place already. It wasn't as though there was much left to see – just a few pictures and some boring old artefacts. Besides, the sooner they got out of here, the sooner they'd be in town watching that film.

He was nearly at the gift shop when he paused, his eye caught by the heading on the last information board. *Village legends*, it read. And beneath it: *Local people say that if you stand on the beach and listen carefully, you can sometimes make out the ghostly sound of church bells ringing underwater. At such times, fishermen refuse to put out to sea, claiming it is a sure sign of a coming storm and fearing for the safety of their boats.*

Joe sighed to himself. Honestly, some people would believe anything. But then who could blame them? Stories like this were probably all the villagers had to keep themselves from dying of boredom.

He pushed his way out of the exit doors.

Sitting outside on the stone wall was his dad, shielding his eyes against a brilliant shaft of sunlight. The rain had cleared away to the east, and in its wake was a vast expanse of bright blue sky.

Joe walked towards him, his face tilted to the sun. Perhaps it was time to give Dad a bit of a break. Perhaps it was time the two of them started getting on again.

Chapter 4

For the rest of the week, the village basked in summer sunshine. Every morning, Joe watched as scores of holiday-makers spilt out of their cars and swarmed on to the beach. Rumour had it the place had never seen such crowds.

Not that they'd spent much time lazing about on the beach themselves. What with boat trips and crabbing expeditions and visits to the cinema, Joe's feet had scarcely touched the ground. Since that first morning in the village museum, he hadn't been bored even for a second.

Things were loads better between him and Dad, too. They'd actually started talking to one another properly; not about Mum or anything like that, but about pretty much everything else. The holiday had turned out to be a great success.

His dad was packing up the car on their last afternoon when Joe came and stood beside him.

"Dad?" he said. "D'you mind if I go down to the sea for a few minutes? Not to swim or anything. I just want to hang out for a bit."

His dad glanced up from the boot.

"Sure," he said, "good idea. I'll come and give you a yell when I'm ready to go."

Joe set off down the path to the beach, stopping only when he reached the water's edge.

It looked like the weather was on the turn again. Just as on their first day, a cluster of black clouds was gathering on the horizon and a stiff breeze was blowing.

He took off his trainers and threw them on to the shingle behind him. Perhaps he'd paddle about for a minute or two. It would be good to feel the sea on his skin before the long journey home.

Rolling up his jeans, he inched forwards, digging his feet into the pebbles.

It was OK, this place, really. His mum had been right to like it so much. There was something about it, something that made him feel relaxed and free. Maybe he'd ask Dad if they could come here again – and maybe next time they could spend more time in the village itself.

He listened to the waves crashing against the shore.

And then he stopped still.

In the distance he could hear something familiar:
the same sound he'd heard when he'd come down here
on their first evening.

Joe took another step forwards, straining his ears for the whisper of music on the buffeting wind. He took another step ... then another. And suddenly there it was, clear as anything: the unmistakable sound of church bells – and they were coming, not from the shore, but from beneath the waves themselves ...

His skin prickled against his clothes.

Hadn't he read something about church bells in the village museum? Something connected to a legend? Yes! That was it! *If you stand on the beach and listen carefully, you can sometimes make out the ghostly sound of church bells ringing underwater.*

Joe stumbled back towards the shoreline, his heart lurching. Back here on the shingle he could hardly hear it, but he only had to crane forwards and there it was again: a deep, steady tolling under the surface of the water.

So the locals were right! There really was something down there. Beneath the rolling waves there was something left of the ancient city after all.

He grabbed his trainers.

Who could blame the fishermen for refusing to go to sea when they heard the eerie sound of the bells? Who would want to be anywhere but a million miles from such a noise?

A voice behind him wrenched him from his thoughts. Spinning round, he saw his dad waving at him from the path at the top of the beach.

"We'd best get going now, Joe! I don't want to get caught up in all the traffic!"

Joe opened his mouth to call his dad down to see if he could hear them, and then he closed it again. What was the point of getting him to come down and listen too? He didn't need someone else to tell him what he could hear with his own ears. The bells were there, proof that something of the past remained, and he was just going to have to accept it.

Slowly, he forced himself to turn back towards
the heaving sea. He crouched down at the water's edge
and trailed his fingers in the frothy spume.

Really, what was there to be so afraid of? The bells
weren't going to do him any harm, were they? They were
a reminder, that was all – an echo from the past. What was
more, they certainly seemed to be doing their job: out
there on the churning grey swell there wasn't a single boat
in sight.

He shut his eyes for a second, trying to commit
the sound of the far-off bells to memory, and then he
slipped his trainers on and walked back up the beach.

"All ready?" his dad asked when they were standing on the path together. He smiled. "No other last minute requests?"

Joe glanced up and met his gaze. "Actually," he said, "there was one thing."

He turned back towards the sea and began to pace in big strides down the beach, counting his steps as he went. When he'd reached 20, he stopped and stood very still, staring out at the stormy sea.

His dad came up behind him and laid a hand on his shoulder. "I thought you didn't want reminding?" he asked.

Joe let out a long sigh. "Can we sit down for a minute?" he asked. "Have we got time? What with the traffic and everything?"

His dad squeezed his shoulder. "Forget the traffic," he said softly. "We've got all the time in the world."

They sat down beside one another on the shingle.

"I won't mind if you want to talk about her," murmured Joe, raking his fingers absent-mindedly through the pebbles. "About Mum, I mean. In fact, I think I'd quite like it if you did."

His dad leant into him. "Really?" he said. "Well, that's wonderful to hear." He swallowed. "It – well, it means we can remember her together."

For a time there was silence, save for the gusting of the wind and the pounding of the waves against the shore.

Joe continued to rake through the shingle, his fingers examining the different textures of the pebbles, some perfectly smooth, some jagged and sharp. He scooped up a handful, then spread out his hand, watching as the smaller stones trickled through the gaps in his fingers.

The next moment he was balling his hand up into a fist. "Dad!" he exclaimed. "*Dad!* Look what I've found!"

Unclenching his hand, he held it out between them:
in amongst the rainbow of stones was a tiny golden moon.

His dad reached out and picked it up. "Well, I never!"
he exclaimed, holding the little moon between his finger
and thumb. "Your mum's earring. And after all this time, too."
He shook his head. "I can hardly believe it."

Joe smiled to himself. He closed his eyes, the far-off
sound of the pealing bells still echoing inside his head.

"Well, you'll have to, Dad," he said. "You'll just have to."

The Girl on the Swing

by Leon Rosselson

Chapter 1

He was always running. He ran from shopkeepers annoyed at the faces he made through their windows. He ran from householders whose front door knockers he'd banged.

He ran from his older sister when she announced her determination to teach him a lesson for his rudeness. Now he was running from some boys who lived on the estate. He didn't know what he'd done to upset them and didn't think it was a particularly good idea to stop and ask them.

He skidded round a corner, saw a black door in
the wall and tried the handle. It opened. He slipped
inside, closed the door and pushed against it. If they
tried it, they might think it was locked. Running footsteps
passed in the street outside.

Billy stood still and silent until the sounds of
the chase faded away. He breathed a sigh of relief.
In a little while, he'd be able to slip back into his part
of town without them seeing him.

He turned round to see where he was. The sun was
dazzlingly bright. He saw everything through a haze.
But it was a garden, he could see that.

Not like his garden – his garden was a mess.
By playing football in it, he'd destroyed the flowers
his dad had planted when he'd been keen on
gardening. But his dad didn't seem to care any more
anyway. Since he'd lost his job – or taken early retirement
as he called it – he hadn't set foot in the garden,
even though he had far more free time now. Billy
couldn't understand it. And his mum was working
and had no time for gardening. Yes, his garden was
a mess all right. But this garden – this garden
was beautiful.

It was a walled garden with rose bushes in full blossom on two sides, their scent filling the air. The diamond-shaped flowerbeds were a mass of flowers forming pretty, colourful patterns. A path through the well-kept lawn led to a pond decorated with rocks and water lilies.

He walked towards the pond, hoping to see some fish in it, then stopped and tensed himself. There was a swing hanging from a tree at the back of the garden and there was someone on the swing, someone swinging gently backwards and forwards. He hoped he wasn't going to have to run again. He was tired of running. And this was such a beautiful, peaceful garden. He wanted to stay in it for ever.

He walked slowly towards the swing. Then he saw it
was only a girl on the swing, a girl a little older than him.
Nothing to be afraid of. She seemed to be smiling at him.

"Is this your garden?" he asked.

She didn't answer him, just continued swinging backwards
and forwards. Couldn't she hear him? She was looking
at him as if she knew him, as if she'd been expecting him.
She wore a white dress, and her light brown hair hung down
to her shoulders.

"Whose garden is it?" he asked aggressively.

"You're in trouble, you are," the girl said.

He stared at her, taken aback. "I don't know what you're on about."

"You're in trouble, you are," she said again. "You wait till they catch you."

He felt a sudden empty ache in the pit of his stomach. Fear. Like the fear that he felt when he'd done something bad at home and he knew Dad was going to shout at him. Or worse. But what was there to be afraid of? And who was he in trouble with anyway? He wiped away a tear of sweat running down the side of his nose. His head felt thick. He felt as if he was suffocating. There was something odd about this garden, about this girl swinging backwards and forwards, smiling at him. The sweat was prickly on his forehead. The sweet rose scent was overpowering. He felt nauseous. He had to escape.

Billy turned and ran.

Her voice came floating into his head from a great distance. "You can't keep running away," she said.

Chapter 2

Dad was drinking a cup of tea in the kitchen when Billy got home. He was reading the paper. He was always reading the paper nowadays, Billy thought. And he looked old – his hair was grey and his face was lined. Billy used to think his dad looked quite young. Not any more.

Billy sat down at the kitchen table. "What's for tea?" he inquired.

"Where've you been all day?" Dad asked, without looking up from his paper.

Billy shrugged. "Nowhere much."

Dad put down his paper and looked at him.
"Here, there and nowhere in particular,
is that it, Billy?"

"Sort of," said Billy.

"I hope you haven't been getting into any mischief,"
Dad said.

"'Course not."

"I hope you haven't been knocking on people's doors
and upsetting shopkeepers."

Billy wriggled uncomfortably on his chair. Someone had
been telling on him. But who? His sister, Donna?

Dad sighed. "Your mum's worried about you, Billy."

"Why?"

"We're both worried about you. What are you going
to do with yourself in the holidays?"

"Dunno."

Dad looked at Billy wriggling on the chair, tense
and defiant, and relented. "Look, Billy," he said,
"you're not a bad boy, I know that. A bit mischievous
maybe, but so was I when I was your age. There's worse
than you around, that's for sure. I just want to know
that you're not getting into any serious trouble."

"I'm not," Billy said. "Honest."

"I hope not," Dad said. "Now, I'd better start getting some tea ready before your mum comes home. Do you want to help me?"

Billy shrugged. "Isn't Donna here?"

"She's gone to Julie's."

"Good riddance," Billy said.

Dad turned on him in a fury. "Don't talk about your sister like that! You should think yourself lucky – "

Billy shrank back.

Dad stopped yelling and turned away. "Go away, Billy," he said wearily. "Leave me alone."

He's getting funny in the head, Billy thought to himself as he climbed the stairs to his room. All I said was good riddance. He didn't have to shout at me.

He threw himself on the bed and stared at the ceiling. Dad was always like that nowadays. One minute he'd be nice and friendly, the next minute he'd be yelling. He wasn't like that when he was working. What was wrong with him now? Billy wished it could be like it used to be when they'd been happy together. A happy family. He'd seen it in the photos in the photo album. He loved looking at those photos.

He slid off the bed and tiptoed into his parents' room next door, pulled out a photo album from the bookcase and carried it back to his room. He sat on the bed and opened the pages. There were photos of his mum and dad when they were graduating from university. Mum looked much the same as she looked now, although she was a bit fatter now.

But Dad did look different. He turned the page. These were the wedding photos. Mum looked really pretty. And they were both smiling. And ...

A photo dropped out of the album on to the floor.
He picked it up and looked at it. Where had that come from?
It was a black and white photo of a girl on a swing.

There was a crease across the middle of it and it was
a bit faded but it was, he acknowledged, a good photo.
The camera had caught the girl laughing as she
soared upwards. She looked as if she was about to fly away.
At first, he thought it was a photo of his sister but then
he saw that it couldn't be. His sister wouldn't dress like that,
not in a million years. So who was this girl on the swing?

Billy sat bolt upright as a shiver of recognition and excitement gripped him. It was the same girl, the girl he'd seen in the garden! But it couldn't be. He examined the photo. It looked like the same girl. But why would Dad have a photo of that girl in his photo album?

The front door slammed. Mum must be home. He slipped the photo into his drawer and carefully carried the album back to his parents' room.

Chapter 3

The next morning, when Donna came back from staying with her friend, she found Billy waiting for her. She looked at him suspiciously. "What do you want?" she asked.

He flinched. She was always so irritable with him nowadays. "I want to show you something," he said. "It's important."

"If this is a trick – " she threatened him, as she followed him upstairs.

He opened the drawer, took out the photo and showed it to her.

"Who is it?" she asked.

"I thought you'd know."

She shook her head. "Where did you get it?"

"From the photo album."

"Well, I've never seen it before." She saw the disappointment in his face. "Ask Dad."

"I can't," Billy said. "He'd be angry. He'd shout at me."

"Because you're always upsetting him. You upset everybody."

"It's not my fault," he muttered.

"No, it's never your fault," Donna said. "Anyway, why do you want to know who that girl is?"

"If I tell you, you won't tell anyone?"

She laughed, surprised. "All right. I won't tell anyone. Come on. What's the big secret?"

"I've seen the girl in the photo," he said.

"What do you mean?"

"Yesterday. I was running from some boys on the estate. I ran into a garden. There was a swing at the back of the garden and there was a girl on it. The girl in the photo."

"You're dreaming," she said.

"It was her," he insisted.

She shook her head. "Impossible."

"All right then," he said, "I'll show you."

It was another hot, summery day. They walked along the high street in silence. Billy shot nervous glances in all directions as if on the lookout for enemies. Donna watched him, remembering how she used to hold his hand and take him for walks when he was just a toddler. Her little brother. He'd been a funny little boy. Now he was just a nuisance, always getting into trouble.

They turned into Wellington Street. The houses here were small, the gardens poky.

"You sure you know where you're going?" she asked irritably.

"You'll see," he said.

He ran round the corner into Nelson Road, with Donna lagging behind.

There it was. The brick wall. So the black door was just …

He stopped, baffled. There was no door. But there had to be. This was the place, he was sure of it. This was the wall. He'd run round that corner and found the black door just there. But it wasn't there. It had gone. Vanished. He ran up and down frantically while Donna watched him, a look of irritation on her face.

"I knew you were just making it up," she said.

"I wasn't, I wasn't!" he shouted, tears of frustration welling up in his eyes. "It was here. I know it was. A black door and a garden on the other side."

He jumped up to see if he could touch the top of the wall, but he couldn't. It was too high to climb.

"Let me stand on your shoulders so I can see over the wall," he pleaded.

"I don't think so," she said. "I'm going back home."
And she turned on her heel and walked briskly away.

He watched miserably as his sister disappeared into
the distance. Then he turned and looked again at the wall.
There it was. The black door. Just where he remembered it.
So how come he hadn't seen it just now? It didn't
make sense.

He approached it warily, half expecting it to disappear
again, and tried the handle. It was unlocked. He pushed it
open and stepped inside. The sun was dazzling. He shaded
his eyes and rested his gaze on the mass of colourful flowers.
The sun was burning. The pond looked so cool and inviting,
he was tempted to jump into it. A low laugh diverted him.
His gaze shifted to the trees and shrubs at the back of the
garden. She was there, watching him. The girl on the swing.
The rope around the tree made a squeaking noise as she
swung lazily backwards and forwards.

He walked towards her and planted himself in front
of her. "Is this your garden?" he asked.

She ignored his question. "You're in trouble, you are."

"Why do you keep saying that?" he demanded.

"Who said you could take that photo?"

He was dumbstruck. How could she have known about the photo?

"Why did you take it?" she asked. But she didn't seem at all angry.

Again the pang of fear in the pit of his stomach. Again the strangeness, the heat prickling his body. Again the feeling of being suffocated. Of going under.

Once again he turned and ran.

"You can't keep running away," she sang out after him.

Chapter 4

Billy gobbled down his dinner, scarcely looking up from his plate. He was afraid Donna would tell his parents about the photograph and the garden that wasn't there. But she didn't. Nobody said anything much. Dad told Billy not to eat so quickly. Mum asked Donna why she just picked at her food.

After tea, Mum announced, "I've got three weeks' holiday from next Monday. How about we go to Cornwall – spend some time by the sea?"

"Fine," said Donna.

Billy shrugged.

They spent the weekend getting ready. After lunch on Sunday, as Billy was throwing his clothes into the suitcase, he found in his drawer the faded photograph of the girl on the swing. Was it the girl he'd seen in the garden? If it was, who was she? And why did Dad have this photo in his album?

He decided, he'd go back to the garden. There was still time. He'd take the photo and show it to the girl. He'd make her tell him everything. This time he wouldn't run away.

He slipped out of the house without anyone noticing and set off at a run. Panting for breath, he reached the corner of Nelson Road. Then he walked slowly to the wall and the black door. But there was no black door. In a panic, he ran the length of the wall looking for it. It had gone again. Desperately, Billy tried jumping up to hold on to the top of the wall. He scraped his hands, arms and knees till the blood ran, but the wall defeated him. Across the road, he saw that in each garden was a wheelie bin. He raced across, dragged out a wheelie bin, pulled it over the road and pushed it against the wall. He clambered up on to it. Now he could reach the top of the wall and pull himself up. Now he could stand on the wall and see …

The garden. The colours of the flowers burning brightly in the sunshine. He stood there, basking in the warmth and loveliness of the garden, drinking in its peacefulness. He felt happy, happier than he'd ever felt. Time seemed to stop. He seemed to have been standing there for ever. From the distance he heard a scream.

Then he felt himself falling.

Chapter 5

"Where is that boy?" Dad asked irritably.

Mum sighed. "I didn't even know he'd gone out."

"Perhaps he went back to the garden," Donna said.

"Garden? What garden?"

Donna hesitated. She'd promised Billy not to tell them about the garden, about the girl on the swing. But there wasn't any garden, there wasn't any girl. He'd made it up. So she told them. She didn't mention the photograph. She didn't want to get Billy into any more trouble.

Dad, agitated, asked, "Where is this garden?"

"There wasn't a garden," Donna replied. "Just a wall. Billy said he went through a black door into a beautiful garden – "

"Where was it?"

"Nelson Road."

Dad looked at her, shocked.

"But there wasn't a door," she continued, not noticing Dad's reaction. "He couldn't have been in a garden. I think he just dreamt it."

"I think we'd better go and look for him," Dad said, looking nervous.

There was no sign of Billy on Nelson Road.

"Perhaps he's climbed over the wall," said Mum.

"Too high," Dad said.

"Billy!" Mum called half-heartedly. But there was no reply.

"Billy said there was a black door in the wall," Donna said. "But there isn't."

"There used to be," Dad said quietly.

"When?"

"A long time ago."

"How do you know that?" Donna asked.

"I used to live here. This was my home."

She stared at him. "Weird. Why didn't you tell us? Anyway, there's nothing there now."

"No," he said grimly. "There isn't."

"But – " Donna began.

"It doesn't make sense," Mum interrupted. "We were about to leave for our holiday. Where is he?"

"Maybe he did get over the wall," Dad said. "Let's check with the houses round the corner. Someone may have seen him."

They knocked on the door of the first house they came to. A man in shorts and a T-shirt opened it. "Sorry to disturb you," Dad said, "but is there a way through your garden to the yard at the back?"

"It's our son," Mum butted in. "We think he may have fallen off the wall."

"You're just in time," the man said, smiling. They followed him into the back room.

"Here are his parents," he announced to an elderly woman sitting in an armchair knitting.

Stretched out on the sofa was Billy. He had scratches and smears of blood on his arms and legs and a large bruise on his forehead.

"Billy!" Mum called, running over to him.

"I'm OK, Mum," Billy said.

The elderly woman didn't get up or stop knitting. "My son was doing a bit of gardening for me and heard a shout," she explained.

"He went to see what it was and found the boy lying on the ground. He must have fallen off the wall. My son carried him in here. He was a bit dazed, but he's OK."

"We need to get him home," Mum said. "I'll go and get the car." Donna and Dad sat down to wait.

"Is there a garden over the wall?" Donna asked. "With roses and flowers?"

The woman looked surprised. "No, my dear," she said. "That yard's all concreted over."

"I knew he was making it up," Donna muttered to herself.

Billy seemed his usual self by the time Mum returned. They got him into the car and thanked the woman and her son.

Just as they were driving off, the son ran out. "I nearly forgot this," he said, handing Dad a photograph. "He was holding it when I found him."

Dad looked at the photo and his face turned grey.

"Come on," Mum said, "let's get Billy home."

Chapter 6

When they got home, Mum cleaned his wounds and, despite his protests, made him lie down on the sofa.

"You need to rest," she said. "That's a nasty bruise you've got."

They didn't seem angry with him. That surprised him. Even Donna was sympathetic.

"Aren't we going to Cornwall?" Billy asked.

"We'll go tomorrow," Mum said, "if you're well enough. I'll phone the hotel to explain."

Dad sat by the sofa. "Feeling better now, Billy?"

"Bit of a headache," Billy said.

"I'm not surprised. What were you doing on that wall?"

Billy looked away. "Nothing."

"Tell me, Billy."

Billy looked at his dad. He felt the urge to confess, to tell him everything. But supposing he got angry. Supposing he shouted ...

Dad handed him the photograph. "You were holding this when they found you."

"I found it in the photo album. I didn't mean to take it, Dad."

Dad smiled. "It seems you don't mean anything you do. Why did you take it?"

Billy looked at the photo, at the girl laughing on the swing. "I thought I saw her," he said.

"You saw her?"

"In the garden. I went through the black door. And when I went back, the black door had gone so – "

"You imagined it, Billy."

"No," urged Billy. "I saw her. She was on a swing like in the photo. And the garden was full of roses and flowers. That's why I climbed on the wall. To see the garden again."

"It was a dream, Billy. There's no garden there."

"But I saw it. Why don't you believe me? And I saw the girl on the swing."

"No," Dad said sharply. "The girl's dead."

He knew as soon as he'd said it, as soon as he saw his son sit bolt upright with shock, that now he'd have to tell him everything.

"Listen, Billy," he said. "I'm going to tell you something, something I've never told you or Donna. I don't know if it'll explain anything, but it might help."

Billy lay down on the sofa and closed his eyes.

"The garden you saw, that was where I used to live when I was growing up. There was a door there, painted black. I remember my dad painting it. He looked after the garden, too. He was a first-rate gardener. That's where we lived – me, my dad and mum and my older sister, Rose."

Billy opened his eyes and looked at his dad questioningly.

Dad sighed. "I loved that house and that garden. I've never been as happy since. When I smell the scent of roses, I imagine I'm back there. Well, it all ended one day in late summer. It's a day I'll never forget. It was stiflingly hot. That day I'd had a bit of an argument with my sister, you know how it is."

Billy nodded.

"I think I was jealous. My dad had taken a photo of my sister on the swing and they thought it was so good they were going to send it in for a competition. So, to get my own back, I took the photo and ran off with it. That's the photo you're holding now. I remember as I ran to the gate, she called after me, 'You can't keep running away.' Something like that. That was the last time I saw her. She went inside. A fire swept through the house. An electrical fault, they said. My sister was killed. So was my dad. My mum was at a friend's house so she was saved. If I hadn't run off, I'd have been killed, too. So you see, you couldn't have seen what you thought you saw. It's gone. The garden. The house. My dad. My sister. All gone."

"Did I dream it then?" Billy asked softly.

Dad thought for a minute. "I don't pretend to understand it," he said at last. "That terrible day is buried inside me. Buried so deep I've hardly told anyone about it. Only your mum. And now you. But lately I've thought about it more and more. So maybe you saw the garden – " he struggled to find the right words, "maybe you were seeing it as I might have seen it, as I remember it. You're a lot like me, Billy, when all's said and done."

Billy was silent, trying to take all this in. He couldn't say anything. He didn't know what to say or what to think about Dad's story. But that didn't matter. Dad was talking to him, telling him things, sharing secrets. That was what mattered. He tried to imagine his dad as a small boy all those years ago arguing with his sister just as he argued with Donna. He tried to imagine what it must have felt like to have his dad and sister die like that. It must have been terrible.

There was a long silence. Billy huddled himself against his dad. "Sorry, Dad," he said.

Dad put an arm round him. "I could make our garden beautiful if you'd help me. Would you?"

"All right," Billy said.

Dad smiled. "You're a good lad, Billy," he said. "I know that."

From denial to hope

Denial

It was easier to push anything to do with Mum right to the back of his mind. Somehow it hurt less that way.

Anger

"Dad!" exclaimed Joe. "Will you stop going on about Mum all the time? It's totally doing my head in."

Pain

How he wished she was here, messing about on the beach with him.

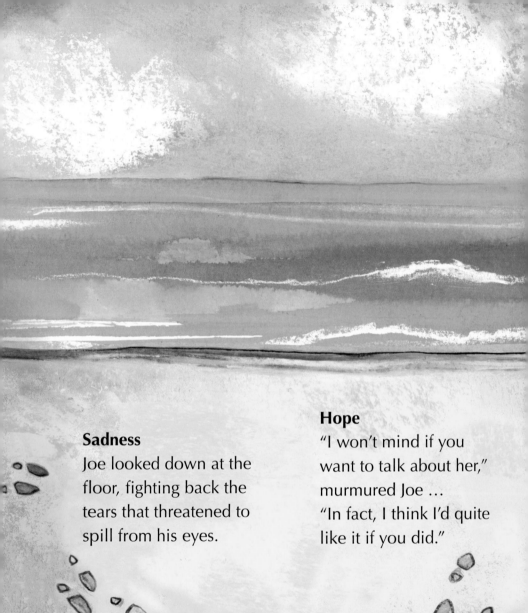

Sadness

Joe looked down at the floor, fighting back the tears that threatened to spill from his eyes.

Hope

"I won't mind if you want to talk about her," murmured Joe …
"In fact, I think I'd quite like it if you did."

Optimism

Perhaps it was time to give Dad a bit of a break. Perhaps it was time the two of them started getting on again.

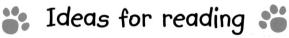

Ideas for reading

Written by Clare Dowdall BA(Ed), MA(Ed)
Lecturer and Primary Literacy Consultant

Learning objectives: understand underlying themes, causes and points of view; sustain engagement with longer texts using different techniques to make the text come alive; use the techniques of dialogic talk to explore ideas, topics or issues; improvise using a range of drama strategies and conventions to explore themes; use different narrative techniques to engage and entertain the reader; set own challenges to extend achievement and experience in writing

Curriculum links: Citizenship: Moving on; Art: A sense of place

Interest words: deserted, illuminated, devastated, buffeting, suffocating, nauseous, recognition, frantically, agitated

Resources: whiteboard, voice recorder

Getting started

This book can be read over two or more reading sessions.

- As a group, discuss who likes reading ghost stories and why. Consider the common features of ghost stories, e.g. the use of descriptive language, the creation of suspense, strange settings.

- Read the blurb. Ask children to consider the image on the front cover and decide which story it's from. Discuss what the stormy setting might represent.

Reading and responding

- Focus on the first story. Ask children to read Chapter 1 silently, noting the emotions that they feel for Joe. Explore how the author creates empathy, e.g. the narrator's insight into Joe's thoughts.

- Ask children to read to p11 and make notes with a partner on what they think the author might be setting up to happen.

- Ask children to finish reading the story, looking for the key themes that occur, e.g. loss, death, memories. Prompt them to make notes on sentences they think paint a strong picture of these themes.